First published 1985
by Running Angel
55 Telegraph Lane East
Norwich
NR1 4AR

Printed in Great Britain by
Rigby Print, Norwich

Design and typesetting by Infoset
Illustrations by Nicola Stevens

Field, Moira
    The lamplit stage.
    1. Norfolk and Suffolk Company of Comedians –
    History
    I. Title
    792'.09426   PN2595.5.E2

    ISBN 0–946600–02–3

Cover illustration from
a contemporary watercolour
of the interior of North
Walsham theatre.

The Lamplit Stage

The Fisher Theatre Circuit
1792–1844

Illustrated from the David and Charles Fisher Collections

By Moira Field

Running Angel   Norwich

Contents

Acknowledgements

First and foremost I wish to thank Kitty Shaw (nee Fisher) and Caroline Fisher Carver, who have allowed me to draw freely on their private collections and answered my many questions about the Fisher family history; and Donovan E. Fisher, who has given me additional information and photographs. I am grateful to Dr Kathleen Barker for reading my manuscript, and to Elizabeth Grice for constant help and encouragement.

For permission to reproduce material my thanks are due to:
- The British Library Board (Songs by David Fisher)
- Viscount Coke, D L (Holkham Hall Archives)
- Frank W Denson (Beccles Town Collection)
- Eastern Counties Newspapers (The Norfolk Chronicle)
- Simon Frey (Photographs of items in the collections)
- L J Hall (Photographs of family portraits)
- National Maritime Museum, Department of Manuscripts (Verses to Horatia Nelson)
- The Wells Centre (David and Charles Fisher Collections)

I am also grateful to the staff of the Colman and Rye Libraries of Local History, Norwich, for their assistance.

Introduction: The Fisher family

There have been many celebrated theatrical families, but not even the most famous of them was more remarkable in versatility and continuity than the Fisher family of Norfolk. Throughout most of the 19th century the Fishers and their Norfolk and Suffolk Company of Comedians spelled glamour and romance in a dozen towns and scores of villages in northern East Anglia, and it was well into the present century before their fame dropped out of the folklore. Even now the Fisher legend is not dead; since 1980 it has been reawakened in Wells-next-the Sea and other towns where the Fishers played by the exhibition of playbills, portraits, and other records of the family's theatrical past, drawn from the private collections of two direct descendants of the first David Fisher.

The known history of the family begins in the 17th century in the village of Hethersett, near Norwich, where they held land, and where several generations continued first as worsted weavers then as farmers. Then, in the middle of the 18th century, one of them moved to Norwich. This was David Fisher, who lived from 1729 to 1782. In Norwich in 1756 he married Mary West of Arminghall and, in the handsome family Bible which he bought and inscribed in 1761, can still be seen recorded the births of their family of ten. The third child and eldest son, David, born in 1760, was destined to establish the famous Fisher company, which, for over half a century, presented an unbroken succession of plays, operas, pantomimes, and other entertainments, in towns all over Norfolk and Suffolk.

The family tree

David I
(3rd of 10 children)
1760–1832

David II
1788–1858

Elizabeth
1790–1808

David III
1816–1887

Walter David IV
1845–1889

David Fisher   m.   Mary West
1729–1782   1730–1819

Charles I
1792–1869

George
1793–1864

Henry
1794–1815

Charles II
1816–1891

George Saul
1833–1907

1 David Fisher I

Because of his importance as founder of the company and of a long line of
actors of his name, this David became known as David Fisher I, though
strictly speaking he was the third in a direct line of eldest sons, all named
David Fisher, running from the 17th century to the present day. He began his

Miniature of David Fisher I (1760–1832) painted by his eldest son.

working life as a carpenter in the building trade, and family tradition has it
that he was also a skilled cabinet-maker and wood-carver and carried out
decorative carvings for several Norwich churches. However, he was
possessed of a fine tenor voice and had a particular talent for singing patriotic
sea-songs, which soon led to his being invited to join the Norwich Theatre
Company as singer, in which capacity he acquired a considerable reputation.
One of his admirers (who chose to remain anonymous) even went so far as to
have sent to him from London each successive volume of Charles Dibdin's
songs as they appeared, and many of these were included in his repertoire for
years to come, along with endless titles on themes national, local, topical or
simply comic: *Famous Victories; If the Frenchmen a Landing Should Win; The
Negociation, or John Bull versus Bonaparte; The Death of Nelson;
Englishmen's Reasons for Becoming Volunteers; Old Bungay; What Are You
At? or, There Never Were Such Times; The New Theatre; The Irish
Yorkshireman; The Wig Gallery;* and many more. After he had been with the

WHEN BENDING O'ER THE LOFTY YARD:

A favourite Song in the

MAN OF ENTERPRISE.

Set to Music and fung by Mr. FISHER

Of the Theatre Royal, Norwich.

Pr. 6.d

Entered at Stationer's Hall.

Printed for and fold by W. Keymer, Colchefter: Sold alfo by Mefs.rs Thompfon No. 75, St Paul's Church Yard.

Song composed by David Fisher I in 1789, while a member of the Norwich Theatre Company.

Norwich company for a while, the manager, Mr Barrett, suggested that he should also try his hand at acting. He made his first appearance as Lubin in *The Quaker,* and soon established himself as a competent character actor. In 1788 he married an actress, Elizabeth Burrell, and both continued to perform with the company for some years. In April 1792, however, after a joint benefit performance on leaving the company, their names disappear from the Theatre Royal's playbills, for at this date David Fisher went into management in partnership with William Scraggs, an already established touring manager leading a troupe that played most of the circuit towns of Norfolk and Suffolk. The following statement in the press announced the new venture.

❝Mr SCRAGGS having resigned to Mr FISHER, of the Theatre Royal, Norwich, the MANAGEMENT of the Company of Comedians, to be by him conducted upon the plan of the first provincial Theatres in the kingdom – for which purpose a compleat set of scenes, wardrobe, etc., have been purchased and a respectable Company of performers engaged – they jointly beg leave to solicit the patronage of the Nobility, Gentry, and other friends of Mr Scraggs in and near the principal towns in the Counties of Norfolk and Suffolk who have hitherto honoured Mr Scraggs, and to assure them that every exertion in their power will be employed to obviate those objections which have in some towns been made to the admission of a Company of Comedians. ❞

Bold words! But justified, for David Fisher turned out to be a brilliant manager, and proceeded to give the public exactly what had been promised.

PROPRIETOR's NIGHT.
By FISHER and Cos. Company of Comedians.
AT THE THEATRE, BUNGAY,
On Thurfday, May 10, 1792,
INKLE AND YARICO,
WITH
THE MIDNIGHT HOUR.
And on the Monday and Tuefday following (being the Fair)
A PLAY and FARCE each Evening,
As will be expreffed in the Bills.
Tickets to be had at the Tunns, King's Head, &c. &c.

Advertisment placed by David Fisher I in the *The Norfolk Chronicle* for 5 May 1782, announcing the opening in Bungay of his first season in management.

2 The Norfolk and Suffolk Company of Comedians

In the David Fisher Collection is one particularly interesting run of playbills, some 200 of them, carefully collected, annotated, and stitched together in bundles, season by season, by some long-dead playgoer in Bungay, whose name is now lost to us. They cover successive biennial visits of the company in the years from 1796 to 1812 – the hey-day of the Fisher-Scraggs partnership – and they speak volumes regarding the endless detail that goes into the making of a successful theatre company. Although these particular bills refer specifically to performances in Bungay, they represent, of course, the repertoire being offered by the company at that time also in a dozen other places scattered between Woodbridge in the south and Wells in the north, Lowestoft in the east and Newmarket in the west.

The company
First, that 'respectable Company of performers' had indeed been engaged. Twenty or more acting members of the troupe are named on each season's bills, led by Messrs and Mesdms Fisher and Scraggs, and including not only David Fisher's two brothers and their wives and various young Fishers and Scraggses, but also a sound core of other experienced actors and actresses, and, equally important, musicians; for music was essential before, during and between all items on the programme. Behind the performers were, of course, as many others: carpenters, scene-painters, stage-hands, property men, prompters, candle and lamp tenders, bill-posters, wardrobe women, money-takers and door-keepers.

Machinery
David Fisher himself was, by his training, a proficient carpenter, and this stood the company in good stead, not only for supervision of regular scene building, but also for the construction of the many special traps, transformations, trick furniture and stage machinery needed, for instance, in pantomime. When Grimaldi's new and popular Covent Garden pantomime *Harlequin and Mother Goose* was put on in Bungay in 1809, it was stated to be 'as closely copied from the original as circumstances will permit of,' and it is no surprise to read on the bill: 'Machinery executed by Mr Fisher.' When, on another occasion, it was announced that

❛After the Farce, Mr Reymes, in the character of Harlequin, will FLY from the Back of the Gallery to the Back of the Stage,❜

it was no doubt Mr Fisher who devised the mechanism for the flight and ensured that he did not land in the middle of the pit.

Scenery
In scenery the company had remarkably high standards. With a large repertoire and the necessity of carrying everything with them from place to place, they must of course have had to make considerable use of stock scenery for the usual forests, caves, cottages, palaces and other scenes of action demanded by the general run of their plays – no doubt the 'compleat set of scenes' mentioned in the partners' announcement. However, specially built and painted scenes for spectacular pieces are soon featured on the bills, and, as time went by, David Fisher adopted the practice of employing a

professional from Drury Lane or Covent Garden, who not only painted scenery but also trained the younger members of the family in this craft. David Fisher's eldest son, David, had early shown aptitude for the work. Already at the age of 17 he is billed as having painted the scenery for the pantomime *Harlequin and Mother Goose,* mentioned above, and two years later was going from strength to strength, as the playbill for *Tekeli* reproduced here shows.

THEATRE, BUNGAY.

By Particular Desire.

On Thursday December 19th, 1811. a Comedy, called

SHE STOOPS TO CONQUER.

Sir Charles Marlow, Mr. G. FISHER
Young Marlow, Mr. FISHER Jun.--Hastings, Mr. SMITH
Hardcastle, Mr. J. FISHER
Tony Lumpkin, (with songs) Mr. FISHER
Stingo, Mr. SCRAGGS
Diggory, Mr. C. FISHER---Serrants, &c.

Mrs. Hardcastle, Mrs. HIGH
Miss Hardcastle, Miss HIGH---Miss Neville, Mrs. G. FISHER.
After which, a Grand Melo Drame, in three Acts, called

TEKELI;

Or, The Siege of Montgatz.

Tekeli, Mr. C. FISHER
Wolf, Mr. SMITH---Maurice, Mr. G. FISHER
Conrad, Mr. FISHER----Isidore, Mr. J. FISHER
Count Carasia, Mr. GARNHAM---Edmund, Mr. SCRAGGS
Bras de fer, Mr. FISHER Jun.----Frank, Mr. HIGH
Officer, Master H. FISHER--Dragoon, Mr. BURGESS.
Alexina, Mrs. FISHER
Christine, (with a song.) Mrs. G. FISHER
Ladies, Mrs. J. FISHER, and Miss HIGH.
Counsellors, Soldiers, Peasants, Attendants, &c. &c.
The Scenery of this interesting and justly admired Melo Drame, Painted by
Mr FISHER Jun. is entirely new, and consists among others of

A Close Wood,

where TEKELI and his friend WOLF lay concealed till surprised and fired
upon by the AUSTRIAN Soldiery.

A distant View of the Castle of Montgatz.

The Bridge of Keben.

The MILLER'S HOUSE

and Celebration of his Daughter's wedding.

Water Mill and Wind Mill at Work.

The Interior of the Castle.

The Council Chamber, Throne. &c. &c.

Concluding with the STORMING of the FORTRESS and the

Triumph of the Heroine of Montgatz.

NB. Second Price admitted as usual.

Costumes

The dressing of the plays, too, was above average standard for travelling companies of the period. David Fisher's grandson, David Fisher III, writing in 1880, recollected:

❛Amongst the things remarkable in the company was the accurate dressing – a complete wardrobe for everything and everybody; but the feature of the Fisher wardrobe was the dressing of old comedies. "Old David" had costly presents of dresses of the last century, and bought largely of gentlemen's servants old swords, wigs in heaps, and some very costly dresses indeed.❜

Printing

In the printing of playbills the Fishers were also self-sufficient, for, although they sometimes used local printers, they had their own portable printing press (duly registered in accordance with the law) and Fisher's brother John and later his son George were both trained as compositors for this work, in addition to being players. Efficient distribution of the bills was of paramount importance, and how thoroughly this was carried out is evidenced by a note which appears from time to time on the bills themselves, as in 1809 in Bungay:

❛If Bills be not left at the Houses of the principal Inhabitants of the adjacent Villages, or within Six Miles of Bungay, Fisher and Scraggs, (as they employ Persons for that Purpose) would esteem it a favour to be made acquainted with such omissions.❜

Both printing and distribution of the playbills must have been continuous activities, for there were four playing-nights a week, all offering different fare, and the exact make-up of each night's entertainment was rarely fixed more than a day or two ahead of performance.

Repertoire

In each two-month season between 30 and 40 different pieces would be given, about a quarter of them 'never before performed here' and some 'never before performed by this company,' no play being repeated 'except by desire'. New pieces must therefore have been in constant rehearsal, with preparation of the necessary new scenes, machines and costumes. Over the years the items offered included everything from Shakespeare (re-written, as was the custom at that time, with extra songs and dances) through the Elizabethan, Jacobean, Restoration and 18th-century drama, to the 'modern' operas, farces, melodrama, pantomimes and spectacles which became fashionable during the period, all interlaced with songs and dances. In other words, whatever was put on in London was brought to East Anglia, often only weeks after its first performance at Drury Lane or Covent Garden.

The repertoire changed gradually, year by year, in conformity with general theatrical tastes, and also extended in its scope as the company grew in experience and David Fisher's children, born and bred to the stage, reinforced its acting strength. Playbills for 22 playing-nights at Bungay in the winter of 1799/1800 show that 20 different main pieces were given.

- Comedies,
    - *The Heir at Law*
    - *Cheap Living*
    - *Lovers Vows*
    - *The Birth Day*
    - *He's Much to Blame*
    - *Laugh When You Can*
    - *The Way to Get Married*
    - *Wives as They Were, and Maids as They Are*
    - *The Will; or, Hypocrisy Exposed*
    - *A Cure for the Heart Ache*
    - *All in the Wrong*
    - *The Wonder! A Woman keeps a Secret*
    - *The Secret*
    - *The Rivals*
- a drama,
    - *The Castle Spectre*
- two tragedies,
    - *Pizarro*
    - *George Barnwell*
- two plays,
    - *The Stranger*
    - *The Horse and the Widow*
- a comic opera,
    - *Abroad and At Home*

Only three were repeated:
- *Pizarro*
- *The Birth Day*
- *Laugh When You Can*

Each main play was followed in a double bill by one of 17 different afterpieces, comprising:
- farces,
    - *The Spoil'd Child*
    - *The Jew and the Doctor*
    - *Fortunes Frolic*
    - *The Irishman in London*
    - *Two Strings to Your Bow; or, The Servant with Two Masters*

The Laſt Night.

NEW THEATRE BUNGAY.

For the BENEFIT of

Mr. and Mrs. SCRAGGS.

On Saturday June 14 1794. (Never Perform'd Here) the laſt New Comedy Call'd

LOVES FRAILTIES.

Written by the Author of the ROAD to RUIN.

Sir Gregory Oldwort,   Mr.   PASTON
Charles Seymour,   Mr.   COURTNEY
Mr Muſcadel,   Mr.   FISHER
Mr Craig Campbell,   Mr.   HINDES
James, Mr. MALLINSON --- Servant, Mr. HUMPHRIES

Lady Fancourt,   Mrs.   FISHER
Nannette, Mrs.   SCRAGGS --- Paulina, Miſs   JESSUP
Lady Louiſa Compton, Miſs   HOWARD
Mrs Wilkins, Mrs.   SELLEE

In the Courſe of the Evening.

The Waggoner, a Comic Song by Maſter SCRAGGS.

A Song call'd [The Days we now poſſeſs] from Collins Evening
Bruſh, by Mr. SCRAGGS.

IMITATIONS.

Of ſeveral well known Performers late of the Norwich Company.
by   Mr.   SCRAGGS.

A Sea Song, [from Ploughing the Ocean] by Mr.   SCRAGGS.

After which the Favorite Muſical Entertainment Call'd

The Poor Soldier.

Captain Fitzroy,   Mr.   STACKWOOD
Patrick,   Mr.   FISHER
Dermot,   Mr.   WORTHINGTON
Darby,   Mr.   SCRAGGS
Father Luke,   Mr.   PASTON
Bagatelle,   Mr.   PRATT
Boy,   Maſter   SCRAGGS

Norah,   Miſs   JESSUP
Kathleen,   Mrs.   SCRAGGS

To Conclude with the Cries of London after the Manner of the Late Ned Shuter,
by Mr.   SCRAGGS, Riding on an Aſs.

Tickets and Places to be had of Mr. J. Dyball, in the Market Place and of
Mr. and Mrs. Scraggs, at Mr. R. Ablet's.

- musical farces,
    Lock and Key
    The Flitch of Bacon
    My Grandmother
    The Padlock
    The Quaker
    The Rival Soldiers
    The Turnpike Gate
    The Farmer
    Rosina
- a musical play,
    The Recruiting Serjeant
- a pantomime,
    Magician; or, Harlequin Everywhere
- a dramatic romance,
    Blue Beard; or, Female Curiosity,
    repeated three times

There were also songs by Mr Fisher and other members of the company, dances (notably a hornpipe by Mr Mallinson, repeated on eight evenings), and a recitation after the play, by Mr Reymes: *Africans Appeal to the Britons for Abolition of the Slave Trade.* The only young Fisher to appear in this season was Miss Fisher, aged nine, who danced with Master Scraggs.

Thirty years on, in 1828, playbills for the Bungay season still offer the same mixture of play and afterpiece with music and dancing, and some of the old favourites, such as the musical farce of *The Turnpike Gate,* are still being played. But the list of the main pieces is now strong in the classics – no longer just *The Rivals* but also *A New Way to Pay Old Debts, Venice Preserved, Macbeth, Othello, Hamlet* and *The Merchant of Venice.* Significantly, the players now include Messrs D, C and G Fisher and their wives (David Fisher's three sons and daughters-in-law), while the small fry are now his grandchildren.

Lines of business
The advantages to a manager of having such a stock of different pieces to present virtually on demand are obvious. Not only could he tempt back a numerically limited audience to visit the theatre again and again by offering endless variety of fare, but he could keep his finger on the pulse of his public and suit each presentation to their moods and wishes. But what of the players? How could a company of some two dozen actors possibly be prepared to perform 30 or 40 different pieces in the course of seven or eight weeks, not to mention providing incidental music, songs and dances into the bargain? The answer is that the system of the day produced actors who expected to be engaged not to play a specific part but to fill a specific place in a company whose members were equipped between them to put on any play in the repertory, each contributing his or her own acting specialities, or 'line of business'. These 'lines of business' were clearly laid down. The *leading man* played the principal rôles in tragedy and melodrama, *the juvenile,* who might also be the company's *light comedian* played lovers and fine gentlemen, and the *heavy* played weighty characters and villains. The company would also have an *old man,* an *eccentric*

comedian, a *low comedian,* several *walking gentlemen* (playing gentlemen, courtiers, and confidants) and one or two *utility men,* ready to tackle anything. The actresses also had comparable well-defined functions. This meant that the casting of any piece was almost entirely predictable, and, though some lines of business overlapped, and it was also possible for a young recruit to rise through the ranks, at any given time almost all the rôles in the repertoire would be in effect the property of individual players. The management records of Drury Lane of this period contain a list of the parts 'belonging' to their various actors, including Edmund Kean. That he himself took a thoroughly proprietary attitude to his parts is clear from a letter he wrote in 1822 to the manager, Elliston, who had hired a new young tragedian in Kean's absence.

'When I come to London, Elliston,' he writes, 'I open in Richard the 3^d my second character *Othello!!* Hamlet – Lear – & so go through my general cast, if Mr Young is ambitious to act with me – he must commence with *Iago.* – & when the whole of *my* characters is exhausted we may then turn our thoughts – to Cymbeline, & Venice Preserved...'

It follows from all this that any actor worth his salt would have in his head a stock-in-trade of characters that came in his line of business, which could be performed more or less on demand with the help of one or two rehearsals and a little support from the prompter. In a circuit company like the Norfolk and Suffolk Company of Comedians there was the added advantage that most of the plays would be revived half a dozen times in the course of a year and so be kept alive in the player's memory.

3 The audience

It was customary to give only four performances during the week (the intervening evenings being often devoted to musical or other parties at the big houses of the neighbourhood) but each playing night was a marathon. The actor F C Burton, last surviving member of the Fisher company, who lived until 1917, wrote in his old age:

‘Ordinarily the performances lasted from 7 p.m. to midnight, commencing with a five act tragedy or comedy, followed by a song by the comedian. Then one of the young ladies would dance or sing a ballad, to be followed by a farce, and the evening would conclude with a two or three act melodrama. The members of the company had to be well equipped in all the arts of the profession. They were well supported by the public, and I have seen three Earls in Eye Theatre at one performance. ’

Bespeaks by the gentry
The three earls were no doubt present at one of the 'bespeak' performances which took place 'by desire of' the local gentry, who requested a play of their own choice and made what we should call a 'party booking.' This ensured the management a good lump sum and also attracted others to these gala nights. David Fisher III, the founder's grandson, in his later years recalled these occasions:

‘The theatres were supported by all classes. Plays used to be "bespoke" or, as it was understood, "bespeak nights" took place, when the names of Lords Rendlesham, Berners, Suffield, Heniker, etc. etc., Sir Edward Kerrison, Coke of Holkham, Villebois, etc. etc., would be found at the head of the bills; and the family of the patrons also in the theatre, with large parties from the mansions of the family. In fact the families of the counties from the very highest estate were the constant patrons of the theatre, and I have recollections as a boy of dress-circles filled on occasions by persons of the highest distinction. ’

Carriages
The number of carriages driving to and from the theatre on such occasions called for special traffic arrangements, duly notified through that all-purpose means of communication, the playbill. At Bungay in the early 1800s, the

THEATRE, WELLS.

On FRIDAY, AUGUST 3rd, 1838,

BY DESIRE OF

THE OFFICERS
OF THE COAST GUARD.

Will be performed, for the first time in Wells, Planche's celebrated Comedy, (acted with the most distinguished success at the Theatre Royal, Drury Lane,) called

THE

PATRICIAN
AND
PARVENU

OR, CONFUSION WORSE CONFOUNDED.

Sir Osbaldiston de Mowbray, Bart. Mr. FISHER
Percy de Mowbray, his Son, Mr. LEMMON—Frank Neville, Mr. CHAPMAN
Sir Timothy Stilton, Knight, Mr. C. FISHER
Dick Moonshine, alias Captain the Honorable Augustus Fitz-Moonshine, Mr. FENTON
Ruby, an obsequious Innkeeper, Mr. TWIDDY Bob Dashalong, Mr. G. FISHER
Decorative Painter, Mr. HOLLIDAY

Ellen Rivers, Miss COPPIN—Mary Stilton, Miss C. ATKINSON
Miss Sally Saunders, Mrs. HODGSON.

A HIGHLAND PAS DE DEUX,
BY MISS COPPIN AND MR. FENTON.
SONG—"THE DEATH OF NELSON"—MR. TWIDDY.

After which, (for the) LAST TIME,) the much admired Drama, called, THE

PILOT ;
OR, A STORM AT SEA.

The Pilot, Mr. LEMMON—Barnstable, Mr. FISHER
Captain Boroughcliffe, (a regular Yankee,) Mr. FENTON
Long Tom Coffin, Mr. C. FISHER—Colonel Howard, Mr. CHAPMAN
Serjeant Drill, Mr. F. FISHER—Lieutenant Griffith, Mr. TWIDDY
Master Merry, Mr. HOLLIDAY.—Recruits, Sailors, &c.
Kate Plowden, Miss COPPIN—Cecilia, Miss C. ATKINSON
Irishwoman, Mrs. HODGSON.

In the Course of the Piece, the following Scenery, &c.
ACT 1.

VIEW ON THE SEA COAST.
STORM AT SEA.
PERILOUS SITUATION of the ARIEL.
RESCUE FROM SHIPWRECK.
ACT 2.
SCENE BETWEEN DECKS—VIEW ON THE SEA-COAST
ACT 3.
Marine View.
COMBAT WITH LONG TOM COFFIN AND AMERICAN SOLDIERS.
ACT 4.
DECK OF THE ALACRITY.
RESCUE OF BARNSTABLE FROM EXECUTION.

On Monday, August 6th,
NEW AND POPULAR PERFORMANCES,
BY DESIRE OF
THE RIGHT HONORABLE
EARL AND COUNTESS OF LEICESTER.

The Theatre will close for the Season, on Wednesday, August 8th, with New and Popular Performances.

THEATRE, N. WALSAHM.
NORFOLK AND SUFFOLK COMPANY.

BY DESIRE OF
Mr. and the Honourable Mrs. PETRE.

On THURSDAY, 29th APRIL, 1830,
The celebrated & admired Comic Opera, called the

Barber of Seville.

The celebrated OVERTURE to the Opera, composed by ROSSINI, will be performed.

Count Almaviva, Mr. HARGRAVE,
Doctor Bartolo, Mr. LAMBERT—Figaro, Mr D. FISHER,
Fiorello, Mr. C. FISHER—Basil, Mr. J. FISHER,
Argus, Mr. HOLLIDAY—Tallboy, Mr. FISHER,
Officer, Mr. GEORGE——Alguazille, Mr. WITHAM,
Notary, Mr. HOLLIDAY—Soldiers, &c. &c.

Rosina, Miss HIBBERT—Marcellina, Miss C. POOLE.

In the course of the Opera, the following Music.

Trio, Piano Planissimo - -	Rossini.	Song, An old man would be wooing - - -	Bishop
Duet, Maiden Fair - - -	Particello.	Song, With that bewitching mien, ah! - -	Do.
Song, Lo! the Factotum -	Rossini.	Song, Away, deceiver -	Do.
Duet, Mighty Jove - -	Do.	Trio, Step as soft as Zephyrs	Rossini.
Song, Tyrant, soon I'll burst thy chains - - -	Do.	Finale, Young Love triumphant smiling - -	Do.
Song, Womankind - - -	Bishop.		
Grand Finale to the First Act	Rossini		

END OF THE OPERA.
A Dance, Master and Miss FISHER.

After which, a New Farce, called

MASTERS' RIVAL,
OR, A DAY AT BOULOGNE.

Mr. Aldgate, Mr. J. FISHER,
Sir Colly Cowmeadow, Mr. LAMBERT,
Peter Shack, Mr. C. FISHER,
Paul Shack Mr. D FISHER,
Captain Middleton, Mr. HARGRAVE,
Barnes, Mr. GEORGE—Sentinel, Mr. HIGH,
Robin, Mr. WHITHAM.

Mrs. Aldgate, Mrs. HODGSON—Amelia, Miss HIBBERT
Tibby Postlethwaite, Mrs. C. FISHER.

Places to be taken of Mr. George, at the Theatre, from Ten till One o'Clock.

PLUMBLY, PRINTER,

Theatre, Bungay.

BY DESIRE OF THE GENTLEMEN OF THE

BOOK - SOCIETY

AND THE TUNS' COFFEE - ROOM·

On Wednesday, January 21, 1824,

The Celebrated and much admired Comedy of

The RIVALS!

Sir Anthony Absolute Mr FISHER

Capt. Absolute, Mr. C. FISHER--Faulkland, Mr. D. FISHER

Sir Lucius O'Trigger, Mr. SMITH

Acres, Mr. J. FISHER--David, Mr. G. FISHER

Fag, Mr FRIMBLY

Coachman, Mr. HIGH--Boy, Mr DAY--Servants, &c.

Lydia Languish, Mrs. C. FISHER--Julia, Mrs G. FISHER

Mrs. Malaprop, Mrs HIGH--Lucy, Mrs J. FISHER

End of the Play,

A Favourite SONG by Mrs. Powis,

A Comic Song by Mr. Stanly.

To conclude with the much admired Farce of the

Weathercock.

Tristram Fickle, Mr. C. FISHER

Old Fickle, Mr. GEORGE--Briefwit, Mr. FISHER

Sneer, Mr J. FISHER--Gardener, Mr DACK

Variella, (with Songs,) Mrs. POWIS--Ready, Mrs. J. FISHER

☞ If Bills be not left at the houses of the principal Inhabitants within four miles of this Place, the Manager, (as he employs Persons for that purpose,) will esteem it a favour to be made acquainted with such omissions.

Doors to be opened at ¼ past 5 & to begin at ½ past 6 o'Clock
Tickets to be had at Mrs. Eaton's, Stationer, where Places for the Boxes may be taken from eleven till one each day
NoPlaces can be secured, unless Tickets be taken at the same time.
Boxes, 3s. - Upper Boxes, 2s. 6d. - Pit 2s, - Gallery 1s
Second price, Boxes 2s. Upp. Boxes, 1s 6d - Plt, 1s. - Gallery 6d.
Children under ten years of age, Boxes, 2s. - Pit 1s 6d.
Days of Playing, Mondays, Wednesdays, Thursdays, and Saturdays.
G. Fisher, Printer.

THEATRE, WELLS.

On MONDAY, MAY 30th, 1836;

BY DESIRE OF

Several Families in the Vicinity of Wells,

When will be performed (for the first time in Wells,) the new and highly successful Comedy, called,

MARRIED LIFE.

Mr. Samuel Coddle, (a Gentleman who cannot endure cold,) Mr. C. FISHER
Mrs. Samuel Coddle, (a Lady who cannot endure heat,) Mrs, HODGSON
Mr. Lionel Lynx, a Gentleman who cannot endure to be suspected,) Mr. LEMMON
Mrs. Lionel Lynx, (a Lady who does nothing but suspect,) Miss COPPIN
Mr. Henry Dove, (a Gentleman who cannot endure to be found fault with,) Mr. YARNOLD
Mrs. Henry Dove, (a Lady who does nothing but find fault,) Mrs. FISHER
Mr. Frederick Younghusband, (a Gentleman who cannot endure to be contradicted,) Mr. FISHER
Mrs. Frederick Younghusband, (a Lady who does nothing but contradict,) Miss C. ATKINSON
Mr. George Dismal, (a Gentleman who likes to do as others do, but not to agree with Mrs. Dismal,) Mr. J. FISHER
Mrs. George Dismal, (a Stay-at-Home.)

A Comic Song, by Mr. Yarnold.

Irish Ballad "RORY O'MOOR," by Miss C. ATKINSON.

A Dance, by Miss COPPIN.

After which, (never acted here,) the new popular and laughable Musical Farce, of The

WANDERING Minstrel.

Mr. Crincum. Mr. YARNOLD—Herbert Carol, Mr. FISHER
Tweedle, Mr. TWIDDY—Jem Bags, Mr. C. FISHER
Mrs. Crincum, Mrs. HODGSON—Julia, Miss C. ATKINSON
Peggy, Mrs. FISHER.

Doors to open at 6, and Performance to commence at half-after
Places to be taken of Mr. GEORGE, at the Theatre, from 11 o'clock till 2.
Boxes, 3s.—Upper Boxes 2s. 6d.—Pit 2s.—Gallery 1s.
Second Price, Boxes 2s.—Upper Boxes, 1s. 6d.—Gallery 6d.
Children under Ten, Boxes 2s—Pit 1s. 6d.

NEVILLE, PRINTER, WELLS.

management had come to an arrangement with the inn next door and patrons habitually used 'A Passage for Carriages through the Fleece Yard,' but on Thursday, January 25th, 1809, we learn that something has gone wrong:

‘As the Landlord of the Fleece, on Thursday evening last without any sort of notice, fastened up his Gate leading to the Theatre, though he had pledged himself to the Managers that a free passage should be continued during the Company's stay. They are compelled to entreat those Ladies and Gentlemen who attend the Theatre in Carriages to Drive by the Hill's Road, which they will have lighted for that Particular Purpose.’

Whatever the rights and wrongs of the row, the emergency can have lasted only for two nights, as Saturday, January 27th, was in any case the last night of the season. On the company's next visit, in 1811, the playbills bear their customary message: 'NB. A Passage thro' Fleece Yard.' At David Fisher's new theatre in Broad Street, opened in 1828, a one-way system seems to have become necessary:

‘It is respectfully requested, that Carriages will set down and take up with the Horses' heads towards the Market-Place.’

Payments for bespeaks
Records of the payments made for 'bespeaks' are rare, but in the Cash Books in the archives of Holkham Hall are entries of payments made to the Fishers which indicate that £10 was the usual sum paid by Lord and Lady Leicester when they themselves attended Wells Theatre with a party, and £5 if only the servants were present. As Wells theatre held £50 in all for a capacity audience, these bookings must have been very welcome. Not only did they guarantee substantial receipts, but the presence of the gentry was doubtless an added attraction for other playgoers, though on occasion it might provide less welcome competition during performance. When Nelson's daughter Horatia went to the play in Wells in 1820, an admirer wrote:

‘With you in vain for Fame a FISHER tries,
You conqu'ring win all hearts and charm all eyes —
You steal attention from the Actor's skill,
The play forgot, you captivate the will —
In you transcendently becoming shine
The genuine virtues of the Nelson line!’

An exaggeration, maybe, but a very possible diversion of attention, considering that in those days the auditorium would be as brightly lit as the stage itself.

It is not only the gentry who figure on the playbills as patrons of 'bespeak nights.' Others include local societies, clubs, schools, masonic lodges, stewards of the races, coastguards, army officers quartered in the town, individual local big-wigs, or simply the 'Ladies' or 'Gentlemen' of the neighbourhood.

Stage replica of a masonic apron of the Unanimity Lodge, North Walsham, worn by George Fisher (1793–1864) on the occasion of the 'bespeak' performance announced in the playbill opposite.

Freemasons' bespeak

One of the items in the Charles Fisher Collection relates directly to a 'bespeak night,' in this case 'at the desire of' the Worshipful Master, Officers, and Brethren, of the Unanimity Lodge of Free and Accepted Masons in North Walsham. It is a replica, meticulously hand-sewn in cream silk, with a red and blue appliqué border, of the masonic apron then in use by the Unanimity Lodge. The procedure on such an occasion was for the members of the lodge to assemble on stage in masonic clothing and sing one or two masonic hymns before taking their seats to watch the entertainment of their choice. The playbill reproduced here shows that, on the evening in question, the 18th of April, 1836, the singing was led by Brother G Fisher, David Fisher's third son, and it is in his branch of the family that both apron and playbill have been preserved. The apron is of silk, not leather, the 'triple tau' emblem on it is worked in sequins, not gold wire, and it lacks the customary tassels; it is, in fact, obviously a theatrical replica, made no doubt for use on stage, where it would have looked convincing enough in the light of the oil lamps. The matching blue and red sash preserved with it, however, is an authentic woven silk sash of the Unanimity Lodge of the time, apparently belonging to George Fisher. Probably his also was another family heirloom, a small silver mug with the initials G.F. and masonic insignia engraved on it, the workmanship, according to family tradition, of David Fisher I. Masonic records show that both George and his elder brother David were at one time secretaries of the Unanimity Lodge. The connection of the Fishers with lodges in more than one of the circuit towns reflects the reciprocal interest between theatre and freemasonry in East Anglia at this period. Norwich even had a Theatrical Lodge, which seems to have moved with the company on its travels.

Sash of the Unanimity Lodge of Freemasons, North Walsham, belonging to George Fisher.

Theatre, North Walsham.

On Monday, the 18th of April, 1836,
BY DESIRE OF
The Worshipful Master, Officers, and Brethren, of the
UNANIMITY LODGE
OF FREE AND ACCEPTED MASONS.

Previous to the Play

The Worshipful Masters, Officers, and Brethren will appear
on the Stage in Masonic Custome, and with appropriate
Regalia—When will be Sung

"*Arise and Blow thy Trumpet Fame.*"
AND THE
ENTERED APPRENTICE'S SONG,
BY BROTHER FISHER.
ASSISTED IN CHORUS BY THE BRETHREN.

Morton's much admired Comedy, called,

SECRETS
WORTH
KNOWING.

Greville, Mr. LEMMON—Egerton, Mr. BELFOUR—Rostrum, Mr. FISHER,
Undermine, Mr. J. FISHER—April, Mr YARNOLD,
Plethora, Mr. C. FISHER—Nicholas, Mr. TWIDDY—Valet, Mr. HOLLIDAY,
Cook, Mrs. HODGSON.
Mrs. Greville, Miss C. ATKINSON—Rose Sidney, Miss REES,
Sally, Mrs. FISHER.

A SONG, MISS C. ATKINSON.
A Comic Song, by Mr. YARNOLD.

After which, (never acted here,) the new celebrated Musical Farce, called,

TAM
oShanter

Tam O' Shanter, Mr. C. FISHER—Souter Johnnie, Mr. J. FISHER,
David, Mr. YARNOLD—Rhoderic, Mr. LEMMON,
Dame Shanter, Mrs. FISHER—Jeannie, Miss C. ATKINSON,
Maggie, Miss REES—Mrs. Macclewee, Mrs. HODGSON.
Witches, Peasants, &c.

In the course of the Piece the following Vocal Performances:

Song,—" O Logie o' Buchan,"
Witches Chorus,—" Tyrant! Tyrant! know thy doom."
Song and Chorus,—" Green grow the Rashes O!"
Glee,—" Good night to ye."
Recitativo,—" The Spirits 've wha ride on high."
Finale,—" Gude Friends around."

On WEDNESDAY the 20th April, the Benefit of
Miss ATKINSON and Mr. BELFOUR.
On THURSDAY, the 21st, the Benefit of
Mr. J. FISHER and Mr. LEMMON.
On SATURDAY, the 23rd, the Benefit of
Miss REES and Mr. YARNOLD.

PLUMBLY, PRINTER, N. WALSHAM.

4 The finances

Seat prices were quite high. A Bungay playbill of 1806 advertises them as:

❝Boxes 3s. Upper Boxes 2s.6d. Pit 2s. Gal.1s. Children under ten Years of Age, Boxes 2s. Pit 1s. 6d. Gal.1s. Second Price to Boxes 2s. Pit 1s. Gal.6d.❞

The box prices refer, of course, to seats (on benches) in the boxes, not to entire boxes. Some time later, when David Fisher had built new and improved theatres, seats in the boxes rose to 3s 6d or even 4s.

❝At these prices,' wrote David Fisher III, 'the theatres variously held from £50 to £70. The prices during only the very last few years were lowered, but never under 3s., 2s., and 6d.❞

Half-price

The 'Second Price' referred to the custom prevailing at that time of admitting a second wave of playgoers half-way through the evening, at a reduced charge. These comprised those who could not afford the full price, those whose work did not release them in time to get to the theatre by the opening hour (5.30 for curtain-rise at 6.30) and those who preferred to forego the main piece of the evening in favour of the frothier delights of the afterpiece. In a double bill the time of admittance for Half-price was self-evident, but for a triple bill presented at Bungay in 1804 the time was made explicit on the playbill: 'Half-price admitted, End of First Act of SIXTY-THIRD LETTER,' this piece being the musical farce which made the middle section of the entertainment. There were occasional exceptions to the Half-price concession, when the cost of a new pantomime or other spectacular afterpiece justified the managers in asking Full-price only, at least for its first two or three performances. So, on January 2nd, 1800, when the Dramatic Romance *Blue Beard* was put on in Bungay, the playbill announced:

❝The Public are respectfully informed that on account of the very great expence attending the performance of the after-piece, No Half-price can be taken.❞

The same message is carried on the bill for January 23rd, but by the third performance, on February 15th, it is 'Half-Price as Usual.' No doubt by this time some of the investment in the piece had been recovered and, its novelty having worn off a little, it was time to go for the more modest receipts accruing from the regular Half-price audiences

Salaries

Against receipts had to be set expenses, an important item of which was the actors' remuneration. In the first half of the 18th century, provincial theatre companies had worked on the sharing system, the profits after expenses being divided out nightly, even down to the remains of the candles. The Fisher company, however, seems from the beginning to have adopted the more up-to-date salary system. We have no records for the earlier years, but for the period from 1832 to 1842 there survives in the family collection a week by week account of the actors' salaries. From this we learn that the rates then ranged from £2 for the manager and £1 5s for leading players down to 15s or 14s for more lowly members of the troupe, with joint salaries for man and wife. Children of the family, though appearing as pages, young princes, etc, from an early age, were not paid until they could be accounted useful actors. In 1833, for instance, one of David Fisher's grandsons, who had been appearing on the bills

NEW THEATRE, BUNGAY.

NORFOLK AND SUFFOLK COMPANY.

THE BENEFIT OF

MR. LAMBERT & MISS FRY.

On THURSDAY, 17th APRIL, 1828,

Shakspeare's much admired and celebrated Tragedy of

OTHELLO,

THE MOOR OF VENICE.

Duke, Mr. GEORGE—Othello, Mr. D. FISHER,
Iago, Mr. C. FISHER—Brabantio, Mr. BARRY,
Cassio, Mr. LAMBERT—Roderigo, Mr. WILKINS,
Antonio, Mr. J. FISHER,
Lords, Senators, &c. Messrs. IFE, BROOKE, HOLLIDAY, &c.
Desdemona, Miss FRY—Æmilia, Mrs. HODGSON.

Song, ' Kitty Clark,' written and to be sung by Mr.
LAMBERT.

Duet, ' *Tell me where is Fancy bred*,' Mrs. D. FISHER and
Miss HIBBERT.

A Dance, Master and Miss FISHER.

Song, ' The New Theatre,' written and to be sung by
Mr. LAMBERT.

After which, the favourite Melo Drama of

THE GALLEY SLAVES.

Henry, Mr. C. FISHER—Bonhomme, Mr. WILKINS,
The Unknown, Mr. D. FISHER—La Route, Mr. J. FISHER,
Basil, Mr. LAMBERT—Felix, Mast. D. FISHER.

Louise, Mrs. C. FISHER.

Villagers, &c. &c.

Boxes 3s. 6d.—Up. Boxes 2s. 6d.—Pit 2s.—Gallery 1s.
Second Price, Boxes 2s.—Up. Boxes 1s. 6d.—Pit 1s.—Gal. 6d.
Children under Ten, Boxes 2s. 6d.—Up. Boxes 2s.—Pit. 1s. 6d.

J. R. AND C. CHILDS, PRINTERS, BUNGAY.

THEATRE, WELLS.

On SATURDAY, JUNE 18th, 1836,

FOR THE BENEFIT OF

Miss COPPIN and Mr. YARNOLD.

Will be performed the much admired Comedy, by Moncrief, called

JOCONDE;

Or, The Festival of the Rosiere.

Prince of Provence, Mr. BELFOUR—Joconde, his Friend, Mr. FISHER
Baillie, Mr. YARNOLD—Lucas, Mr. C. FISHER
Bertrand, Mr. TWIDDY—Hugo, Mr. HOLLIDAY
Soldiers, Servants, Attendants, &c.
Countess Matilde, betrothed to the Prince, Mrs. FISHER
Edile, betrothed to Joconde, Miss C. ATKINSON
Jeannette, Miss COPPIN—Louise, Mrs. HODGSON——Villagers, &c.

A Comic Song, by Mr. Yarnold

A DANCE, BY MISS COPPIN.

After which, (FOR THE ONLY TIME,) the interesting Musical Drama, called

PAUL

AND

VIRGINIA.

Paul, Mr. FISHER—Captain Tropic, Mr. TWIDDY—Diego, Mr. J. FISHER
Antonio, Mr. BELFOUR—Dominique, Mr. YARNOLD
Alambra, Mr. LEMMON—Sebastian, Mr. C. FISHER—Soldiers, Sailors, &c.
Virginia, Miss COPPIN—Jacintha, Miss C. ATKINSON
Mary, Mrs. FISHER—Villagers, &c.

In the course of the Piece the following Songs, Duets, &c. will be sung.

DUET—"See from Ocean rising,"
GLEE—"Haste my Companions,"
SONG—"When the Moonlight's o'er the deep,"
SONG—"Our Country is our Ship d'ye see,"
SONG—"Boldly I come,"
SONG—'O could my fault'ring tongue impart,"
CHORUS—"O blest for ever be this day,"
SONG—"The wealth of the Cottage is Love,"
CHORUS,—"What sounds strike my ear,"
CHORUS—"Hour of Terror,"
FINALE—"Strains of joy,"

And in the course of the Piece the following Scenery,

ESCAPE OF ANTONIO'S VESSEL AFTER

THE CAPTURE OF VIRGINIA.

GRADUAL CHANGE FROM CALM AND SERENE WEATHER TO

STORM AND TEMPEST,

WITH THE WRECK OF ANTONIO'S VESSEL,
And Rescue of Virginia by the Slave Alambra.

Two sheets from the salaries list of the Fisher Company, kept from 1832 to 1842.

for some time and must have been at least 16, is noted in the salary list as follows: 'Fred^k Fisher (Till now had never received any) – 14s.' The total bill for salaries fluctuated between £17 and £21, according to circumstances.

Benefit nights

In addition, 'benefit nights,' on which the members of the company in turn took the profits after deduction of management expenses, augmented the weekly salaries. There survives a fascinating vellum-bound notebook in which David Fisher's third son, George, recorded his own and his wife's benefit receipts from 1823 to about 1839. It is of especial interest in that it shows the gross takings as well as his own share. At North Walsham, for instance, on November 6th, 1823, £26 4s was taken, of which George Fisher's share was £10 12s. On some occasions, when takings were very low, the entries are annotated with comments on the weather ('Incessant Rain'), competition ('Rain and 2 Balls'), or even dirty work at the box office ('Many in without paying! Rascally'). According to their standing in the company, actors would either have an individual benefit, or share one with another player, once in each season. In either case it behoved the beneficiary to rally friends and patrons to the performance, and in some cases special tickets were printed for the occasion. There is in the David Fisher Collection one such ticket, for 'Mr and Mrs D. Fisher.' Benefit nights were almost as important as salary to an actor; a run of successful benefits could double his year's earnings.

Benefits for the poor

Benefit nights were sometimes held not for the benefit of the company but for some charitable purpose, often for the relief of the poor of the district or of small debtors in the local gaol. While it is no doubt true that this kind of gesture stood the company in good stead with the theatre licensing authorities, it was nevertheless a sincere charitable act, meeting a real need. Certainly in Beccles in 1814 a benefit night of this kind was recognised by one of the chuchwardens as a 'spontaneous act of Charity.' He records the event as follows:

❛On the 26th Jan 1814 Mr Fisher's Company of Comedians then at Beccles performed a Play called "The West Indian" for the benefit of the Poor resident in the Town, when the total receipt of the Evening amounting to £18.12.0 was paid by the worthy Manager to the Churchwardens, who distributed 1480 three penny Loaves of Bread, which proved a great Relief to upwards of 1300 Persons at a very inclement Season. ❜

THEATRE, BUNGAY.

Fisher and Scraggs's Company.

For the Benefit of

THE POOR.

Tuesday, Dec, 22nd, 1801, the Comedy of

THE JEW.

Sheva, Mr. PASTON
Sir Stephen Bertram, Mr. MORETON
Frederick, Mr. REYMES—Charles, Mr. WARD
Saunders, Mr. MANN
Jabal, Mr. FISHER—Waiter, Master SCRAGGS

Mrs. Ratcliffe, Miss NEWMAN
Eliza, Mrs. FISHER—Dorcas, Mrs. SCRAGGS
Mrs. Goodison, Mrs. HIGH

End of Act IV,
A Song,—"The Blue Bell of Scotland," By Mrs. WARD.
End of the Play,

A Song, by Miss Starmer.

After which a Farce called

WAYS and MEANS.

Sir David Dunder, Mr. PASTON
Random, Mr. REYMES—Scruple, Mr. WARD
Paul Peery, Mr. SCRAGGS
Tiptoe, Mr. FISHER
Waiter, Mr. MANN
Lady Dunder, Miss NEWMAN
Harriet, Mrs. WARD—Kitty, Mrs. SCRAGGS

The entire Receipt of this Night, will be appropriated by Fisher, & Scraggs, to
the above purpose.

Doors to be opened at Half-past Five and to Begin at Half-past, Six o'Clock.
Boxes, 3s.—Pit, 2s.—Gallery, 1s
Tickets to be had at the Inns, of, Mr. Fisher, Mr. Scraggs and of Mrs. Eaton.
of whom Places for the Boxs may be taken
Days of Playing,—Tuesdays, Thursdays, and Saturdays.

Vellum-bound notebook in which George Fisher (1793–1864) noted the takings for his and his wife's 'benefit' performances from 1823 to 1839.

The Town Hall archives preserve a list of all the persons who received bread from this gift, the number of persons in each family, and the number of loaves received in each case. The amount of bread was apparently sufficient for all comers, for, a first distribution not having exhausted the gift, a second announcement gave

'Notice to some Poor Persons residing in Beccles, as were not relieved on Sunday last, that the Churchwardens will attend at the Town Hall on Wednesday next, at 4 o'Clock in the Afternoon, to distribute the remainder. '

It was in fact a not inconsiderable sum of money that was given – the equivalent, after all, of the whole acting pay-roll for a week.

Management costs
Management costs did not end with the players. Other personnel had to be paid; the theatre or other building used as such had to be rented, heated and lit; new costumes, wigs, hats, swords and stage properties were constantly needed for new pieces; timber, canvas and paint were required for the scenery; paper and printer's ink for the playbills and tickets; and there were incidental services and goods to be paid for in each town they visited. David Fisher's businesslike approach to these last items is indicated by a notice inserted in a Bungay playbill in 1823:

'ALL PERSONS concerned for or in the THEATRE, are requested to take notice that the Manager will not hold himself responsible for any Demand whatever, for Goods, Materials, &c. &c. unless the same be caused by an order bearing his hand-writing. And to prevent error, Bills of every denomination are desired to be sent in every Saturday for their discharge. '

Transport
Finally, there was the cost of transport. At the end of the season the whole company moved on to the next town, travelling over long and difficult roads with vast quantities of impedimenta – scenery, stage properties and costumes – all conveyed in huge, horse-drawn waggons. In the late 18th century Arthur Young described some of the Norfolk turnpikes in winter as 'ponds of liquid mud, with a scattering of loose flints, just sufficient to lame any horse that moved near them,' and they were not improved by the passage of the heavy waggons. The steward of the Holkham estate of Coke of

Norfolk, writing to a tenant farmer at the end of the summer of 1818, directing him to repair a road running through his land, says: 'I know that at present this road appears fair to the Eye, but is superficially so, and from there being scarcely any hard material upon it, it is always most dreadfully cut up in Winter by the heavily loaded narrow wheeled Waggons, which pass over, or rather through it.' In spite of this, there were never more than from two to five days between finishing in one town and opening in the next. We have no record of what David Fisher expended on cartage and on loading and unloading, but we know that the Norwich company on circuit, travelling similar routes, spent about £300 a year. In winter they used three waggons each holding six tons of equipment and drawn by teams of six horses, though in summer better weather and drier roads allowed them to reduce the number of waggons to two. The Norfolk and Suffolk Company is said to have used the same number and type of waggons, but family tradition adds that David Fisher was able to make a considerable saving in the cost by borrowing the horses for each journey from members of the family who had remained on the land as farmers.

A personal view is given by David Fisher II, writing from Woodbridge to his uncle Thomas Sadler, a Norwich grocer, on February 23rd, 1825

'Dear Uncle,
You know very well you never behold my beautiful handwriting but when I want to Bother you about something or other – The present is no exception to the above Rule – But I am in a hurry therefore to Business – I am going to exhibit my sweet person on the *Lynn Boards next Monday* – It will be necessary that I should have the wherewithal to decorate, etc etc. I have therefore sent off a large Box this morning per carrier to Norwich – he puts up at the Pope's Head, St. Peter's – at least so they tell me – Now they also tell me there is a waggon from the aforesaid Pope's Head to Lynn on the Saturday Afternoon – Now my request to you is that you would be so kind as to see that the said Box is safely deposited in the aforesaid Lynn Waggon, provided it can be conveyed to Lynn and arrive there to a certainty on the Monday by two or three o'clock – that is to say, in time for me to get my dress out and air it in time for the Evening Performance. Unless the Waggoner can faithfully promise that he always arrives at Lynn at the said time I know not what to do!

I must have my box there – that is a *sine qua non!* It must be there – This the most inconvenient place in the whole circuit for conveyances, but I must have my Box – Therefore if the said Waggoner does not arrive at Lynn in time will you form some bargain with him to send a man and cart (with a horse in it) on to Lynn from some (the nearest place he can to Lynn) place where it stops? I know of no other plan. I must have my Box, and so I must not mind a guinea or two if it must be so, for I must have my Box. I have no doubt but you understand my meaning though it is rather hastily expressed. You understand the carriers etc etc. Therefore I will leave the Business to your superior judgement.

I am sorry to give you the trouble, but I have no other means of at all ensuring the arrival of my goods and Chattels in time for the Market. Adieu. All well. Love to all. Yours ever obliged and all that and everything in the world and so forth.

D. Fisher, Junr.'

5 The circuit

Circuit life was indeed strenuous. It took about two years to make the complete round, with a season of some two months in each town, preferably arranged to coincide with assizes, fairs, races or other crowd-pulling events. The two-month period was not arbitrary. Not only was it about the right length of time to take up the available audience in each catchment area, but 60 days was also the maximum period for which, by the terms of the 1788 Theatre Licensing Act, magistrates were empowered to allow travelling companies to perform in one place. Among the small green-backed notebooks in which the Fishers recorded their business is one listing the magistrates and clerks of courts of the various towns in which they played. Apart from a very occasional short pause (Passion Week, the Norwich Music Festival, or a rare week or fortnight's vacation) the round was endless. Births, marriages and deaths hardly broke the routine.

Puritan opposition

In their announcement of their partnership in 1792, David Fisher and William Scraggs are at pains to assure the public that

❝every exertion in their power will be employed to obviate those objections which have in some towns been made to the admission of a Company of Comedians. ❞

This no doubt refers to charges of immorality made against the stage by puritanical groups and sects active at that time, as indeed at many others. The manifest respectability of the Fisher-Scraggs company and the high standard of their repertoire probably saved them from objection by all but the most fanatical opponents of the theatre, but they did encounter occasional opposition. In 1793, after hearing of 'malicious aspersions' raised against the company in Eye, 40 playgoers in Walsingham felt it incumbent upon them to write to the Eye newspaper in their defence. In the course of their letter they give Fisher and Company's Comedians the following testimonial:

❝We, the undersigned residing in or near the parish of Little Walsingham, in Norfolk, do, in justice to the above company declare, that during their stay in Walsingham, which has been frequent and for many weeks together, they have performed with much credit to themselves and satisfaction to their auditors; and that they have always conducted themselves in a manner that has gained them general attention and respect... ❞

They add that

❝this declaration is made without any application whatever from Fisher & Co. and even without their knowledge, but purely as a mark of our good opinion of them. ❞

In Halesworth in 1808 there was a much bigger row. The Methodist minister, the Rev J Dennant, started it off with a sermon against playgoing, preached in advance of the company's arrival for their autumn season. The physician, Dr Morgan, replied in print, and the attorney, Mr Jermyn, joined in, also on the side of the players. Then a veritable pamphlet war broke out, the rival factions using the town's two rival printers for their attacks and counter-attacks, some of them in verse. Dennant's fulminations against plays for their 'love intrigues, blasphemous passions, profane discourses, lewd descriptions and filthy jests' seem, however, hardly to have touched

The circuit

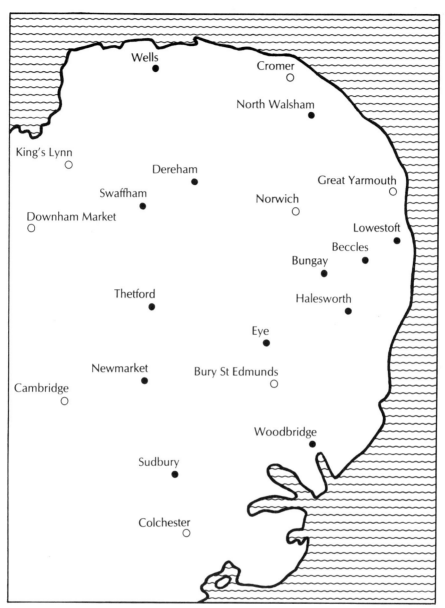

Wells

Cromer

North Walsham

King's Lynn

Dereham

Great Yarmouth

Swaffham

Norwich

Downham Market

Lowestoft

Beccles

Bungay

Thetford

Halesworth

Eye

Newmarket

Bury St Edmunds

Cambridge

Woodbridge

Sudbury

Colchester

Towns visited in 1834
Bungay
North Walsham
Wells
Dereham
Swaffham
Newmarket

Towns vistited in 1835
Woodbridge
Sudbury
Eye
Lowestoft
Beccles
Halesworth
Beccles

Key
● Circuit towns
○ Others not on the circuit

THE PAMPHLETS.

TUNE.—" OLD HOMER."

IF you please, Sirs, might I be so bold as to say,
For I fancy I've somehow been missing my way,
Is this pray the *playhouse*, 'bout which there's a pother,
Or have I mistaken *this* house for *that* other.
                              Tol lol de rol, &c.

'Tis *but* a short time, since I came to this town,
From Norfolk you see, and a poor simple clown;
And so in a poor simple way I will sing,
Of what I have heard, till it made my ears ring.
                              Tol lol, &c.

When *first* I came here, the good town was all quiet,
And nobody thinking of breeding a riot;
Now then 'tis no wonder that I am amazed,
When I see all the people with pamphlets half crazed:
                              Tol lol, &c:

At first one came out in a moderate way,
And argufied all about seeing a play ;
Then another of learning brought in such a hawl,
If he that composed, understood it—*that's all*.
                              Tol lol, &c.

I tried at the Swan, and the Ship, and the Sun,
To get some to read it, but as Greek 'twas all one;
And whilst I was wond'ring what it could mean,
Pop—out comes another, that last to explain.
                              Tol lol, &c:

The next was a letter, and sure the inditer
Had gotten by heart, " The Complete Letter Writer;"
For plainly he prov'd, I should find *no bad* seat in,
A house not a mile past the house call'd the Meeting.
                              Tol lol, &c.

Then came an Appeal, and then a Review;
Then Stanza's, and then came the Dunciad too;
But they thicken so fast, that I only can say,
Where we'd one in a week, we've now two in a day.
                              Tol lol, &c:

TIPPELL, PRINTER, HALESWORTH.

Verses written by David Fisher I and sung by him from the stage at Halesworth in 1808, when there was a pamphlet war about the theatre in the town.

‘ ...Mister Fisher and his pretty da'ter,
With Mistress Scraggs, and Mr. Scraggs, et cetera, following a'ter, ’

as one of the protagonists described them. Indeed, when David Fisher himself
joined in with a song *The Pamphlets* (sung from the stage to the tune
of *Old Homer*, and printed as well) he took a less than solemn view of the affair.
'Is this pray the *playhouse*, 'bout which there's a pother?' he sang, affecting the
innocence of a 'poor simple clown' from Norfolk:

‘When *first* I came here, the good town was all quiet,
And nobody thinking of breeding a riot;
Now then 'tis no wonder that I am amazed,
When I see all the people with pamphlets half crazed:
Tol lol de rol, &c ’

End of the partnership
The company remained the Fisher and Scraggs Company for 20 years, but, as
time went by, the Fishers steadily out-numbered the Scraggses, as David's wife,
his two brothers and their wives, and, in due course, his sons and daughter
made their appearance on the bills. Then on February 12th, 1808,
William Scraggs died. A newspaper report of the time records the event:

‘On Friday last died at Beccles, aged 60, Mr William Scraggs, joint manager of
a company of comedians well known in Suffolk. – A man possessed of much
eccentric humour and highly respected as a social companion. ’

His body was attended to the graveside by a torchlight procession, in which the
freemasons joined; on his headstone was inscribed simply: 'To the memory of
William Scraggs, comedian.' His interest in the company passed to his wife, but
four years later she also died, leaving her theatrical property to her son,
Robert Beeston Scraggs, who then parted company with Fisher. After this, the
Norfolk and Suffolk Company of Comedians became solely a Fisher concern.
In March 1812 *The Norfolk Chronicle* reported:

‘The partnership between Messrs Fisher and Scraggs having expired, the
theatre at Thetford was opened for the season under the direction of
Mr Fisher only, with that success which diligence and long-established
integrity merit. ’

That the parting was perhaps not totally amicable is suggested by the fact that
the younger Scraggs billed his own company as The Original Norfolk
and Suffolk Company.

Lowestoft theatre

6 The theatres

By this time David Fisher had established a sound reputation among the theatre-goers of the two counties, and knew exactly which places could be counted on for the best patronage, particularly from the local aristocracy and gentry. According to his grandson, his circuit was based on 'direct communication with people of influence' and he seems to have mixed easily with the gentry and nobility, who are said to have made him and his family welcome guests in their homes. After William Scraggs's death he began to put his managerial judgment to the test. Hitherto he had hired whatever theatre, inn, or fitted-up barn was in use as the existing playhouse. Now he began to build theatres for himself, investing his own money in them and also raising share capital to finance some of the projects.

The first record of his building activites is in a Lowestoft court roll of November 1810, which records his admission 'to a piece of land at Lowestoft, on which he is building a theatre.' It opened in 1812, when a guide book to the town describes it as

'a spacious building,' which 'has lately been erected by Mr Fisher, the proprietor, and the manager of a respectable company of comedians, who at regular intervals pay their devoirs to the inhabitants of Lowestoft and its vicinity.'

That same year, 1812, in Wells-next-the-Sea he replaced the barn that had long served as a theatre there by a new playhouse on a new site. Between 1812 and 1828 he built new theatres or adapted existing ones also in: Woodbridge, East Dereham, Eye, Sudbury, Thetford, Beccles, Swaffham, Newmarket, Bungay and North Walsham. Living accommodation for the company was provided where possible, and at Woodbridge and Dereham he built family homes adjacent to

The Theatre Royal, Dereham

39

the theatre. The Woodbridge house, built in 1814, may well have been the first permanent home David Fisher and his wife Elizabeth ever had. Unhappily, she died there only a few weeks after the opening of this his third theatre, and was buried in Woodbridge churchyard. The Dereham house, built two years later, no doubt as a base at the other end of the circuit, was particularly convenient, being large enough to house most of the company, and having a door leading direct from a recess in the hallway into the wings of the theatre.

The Dereham theatre was the last one to be used as a playhouse. It survived in its original form until the 1930s, when it was remodelled, and was finally demolished in 1977. In Lowestoft the superstructure of the theatre was rebuilt as assembly rooms in the 19th century, but the understage area survives, and the whole is now a community hall. The shells of others still stand, much altered and serving various purposes, in Woodbridge (sale room), Eye (garage), North Walsham (show room), Swaffham (garage), Beccles (store room), and Bungay

Swaffham theatre

(warehouse). In Bungay the pedimented façade typical of Fisher's theatres stands almost exactly as it is shown in a contemporary drawing in the Suffolk Record Office. A similar façade still remains at Thetford, where the parapet was formerly adorned with several large marble busts of Roman emperors (originally brought from Italy by the Earl of Arlington) though the theatre itself has been converted into a private house. Wells theatre, too, became a dwelling, comprising four tenements, with a communal washroom in what had been the stage area, but was pulled down in 1965. Newmarket and Sudbury theatres have also disappeared, though the Suffolk Record Office has drawings of both the interior and exterior of the Sudbury building, showing a style of playhouse different from Fisher's other theatres; and it appears that this was one which he did not in fact build, but adapted from an existing playhouse. At Halesworth he continued to use the existing theatre, which later became a rifle hall and is still used for various forms of recreation.

Design of the theatres.

Fisher's playhouses were simple buildings of modest size (probably capable of holding 300 or 400 spectators) but soundly constructed of brick or stone. The roof sloped down from above the gallery to above the stage, thus making most economical use of building materials. Entrance lobbies, dressing rooms and other utility areas flanked the main structure of auditorium and stage. The auditorium accommodated two rows of boxes, pit and gallery, all furnished with baize-covered backless benches. Most important of all, the stage was of generous proportions and designed always to take scenery of uniform dimensions. The outside covers of a small book entitled, on one cover, *PLANS of Audience Part of Theatres,* and on the other (the other way up) *Order of Scenes. Inventory of Scenes. Inventory of Scenes and Various Articles Left at Different Theatres,* and dated 1832, still survive in the collection. Though the pages are missing and only an index remains on one end-paper, a tantalizing summary on the other end-paper gives the standard dimensions of the scenes, with slight variations at one or two of the theatres, and directions on the spacing of the side wings. That this uniformity lightened the burden of travelling the shows is made clear by David Fisher III in the reminiscences already quoted, when he writes: 'general scenery was conveyed from town to town; but act-drops, curtains, etc., were fixtures.' There was no elaborate machinery above or below stage, though it is clear from the playbills that special effects and machines were made for special productions.

David Fisher himself designed and supervised the building of his theatres, his earlier training as a carpenter and builder serving him in good stead. Most of the interior decoration was in the hands of his eldest son, David Fisher II, who

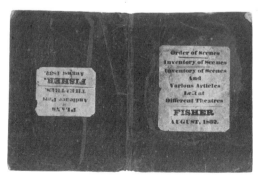

The cover (all that remains) of the green leather management notebook which once contained details of both stage and seating for every Fisher theatre.

Thetford theatre

already had great skill in scene painting and in addition had studied architecture and perspective. The combined talents of father and son produced unpretentious but commodious and elegant theatres, as contemporary accounts bear witness. The following description comes from a press report of the opening of Fisher's second theatre, in Woodbridge, on February 5th, 1814.

Woodbridge theatre

'The Theatre was built by Mr THOMPSON, from a plan, we are informed, of Mr FISHER's, the Proprietor. Its cost is said to have been altogether about 2000l. The form – as to construction rather old-fashioned than new – is judicious; for the size of the house the accommodation is, in every respect, good; and the painting, decorations, &c. are such as to give it a neat, light, and airy appearance. It is calculated to hold from 70 to 80l. The stage, which possesses great depth, is sufficiently large for any scenic representation, not depending on *spectacle* or procession. On each side of the stage are two tiers of boxes, four boxes in each tier; the lower tier having also three centre boxes, at the back of the pit. The pit contains about ten or eleven seats; and the gallery seems well proportioned to the other parts of the Theatre. '

Bungay theatre

The Woodbridge auditorium was lighted by 'Liverpool lamps' – an improved version of the oil lamps which, with candles, were the sole form of lighting in most theatres at this time, and which remained so in the Fisher theatres throughout David Fisher's own life time. In 1836, however, Woodbridge theatre had the distinction of going over to gaslight.

North Walsham theatre.

The exact appearance of the interior of one of the Fisher Theatres – North Walsham, the last to be built, in 1828 – is known to us from two water-colour sketches made by a certain Mr G T Plumbly, host of the Angel Inn in that town, who was also a great friend of the Fishers, and indeed played the violin in the theatre orchestra when the company was in North Walsham. The colour-scheme of the auditorium, painted by David Fisher II, is blue and beige, picked out in white, with decorative gold motifs, which are in fact masonic symbols, further evidence of the family's close connection with the freemasons here. When lit up for performances by oil lamps along the rows of boxes, and candles and lamps from the stage, the whole interior must have gleamed in the soft light. The contrast between the new theatre and the barn fit-up it replaced on the same site was pointed by some lines in the Opening Address spoken by David Fisher's second son, Charles, at the first performance on Tuesday, May 6th, 1828:

' When two years since on this same spot we met,
In cold clay walls, with roof of thatch ye sat;
Then Richard, Richmond marshall'd their proud ranks
On stage no bigger than a mountebank's;
Then Scotland's tyrant barely fought his squadron
In space scarce larger than the witches' cauldron;
Here, as we oft portray'd their furious ire,
The eddy winds damp'd our theatric fire.
Look round, my gen'rous friends, and you'll view
Instead of barn, an edifice quite new;
One more deserving of your lib'ral aid,
One where our Drama may be best displayed.
On spacious stage our harmless combats fight
And Richard be himself again each night. '

Sudbury theatre

Use between seasons

The Fisher theatres seem not to have been used by other companies of comedians. This may appear strange to us now, but a Fisher season in one of the circuit towns was in the nature of a biennial festival, an event for which people saved up, to which playgoers from the neighbouring villages came in waggons decorated with flowers; and for the company to open up their hard-won facilities and goodwill to exploitation by rivals would have been to spoil their own market, precarious enough in any case. They did, however, allow their playhouses to be used on occasion for other types of entertainment. The Wells theatre, for instance, in 1836, was used for a concert and ball in aid of funds for establishing an infant school in the town, and in Woodbridge the Fishers gave permission for a series of concerts to be given in the theatre by the Woodbridge Amateur Music Society, members of the family even sometimes taking part.

Eye theatre

They also let off the ancillary parts of at least some of their theatres in between their own visits. In 1828, when the theatres in both Bungay and North Walsham were opened, playbills for both towns carry advertisments to this effect.

A note on a Bungay playbill of March 29th reads:

'To be Let, and possession had after Easter, the Dressing and other Rooms of the Theatre, together with a good Cellar, &c. &c. Three of the Rooms are 20ft. by 12ft. and four of smaller dimensions. Inquire at the Theatre, or of Mr.Weeds, Earsham Street.'

Similarly, at North Walsham on June 13th, at the foot of the bill appears the notice:

'TO BE LET in several Tenements, Ten Rooms now used as Lobby, and Dressing Rooms of the Theatre. For Particulars enquire of Mr Fisher.'

7 The family

In the heyday of the company there were enough talented Fishers among them
to take up to nine or ten parts in one evening's entertainment; in all, 18 of them
acted on the family circuit. But there was nothing haphazard about the entry of
David Fisher's children into the acting ranks of the company. His sons were
given classical schooling and musical training at a boarding school run by a Dr
Binfield in Whittlesea before serving their apprenticeship on their father's stage,
and even in their earlier years they attended the local schools in at least some of
the circuit towns. The playwright, Edward Fitzball, writing of his own schooldays
in Newmarket, recalls:

❝The young Fishers, the manager's sons, came to our school – didn't I envy
them the possession of the tin daggers which they sometimes stealthily
brought up their sleeves to astound the boys with!❞

The family business
All members of the family acted, danced and sang as a matter of course, and
most of them played a musical instrument as well. David Fisher's brother John
was the company's printer in the earlier days; another brother, George, became
and remained the 'box-book keeper' (what would now be called box-office
manager). Both the brothers' wives were players in the company, George's bride
being already a member of the troupe before her marriage. This George Fisher
came to be billed as 'Mr. George' to distinguish him from his nephew, another
George. By the time David Fisher was building his theatres, his sons also were
fully fledged actors, making their individual mark on the stage and contributing
to the business side of the circuit – David as scene painter, Charles as assistant
manager, and George as printer. In 1827, with the end of his building
programme in sight, he seems to have thought of retiring, for, in an indenture
dated January 31st of that year, he professes himself desirous of retiring from
the management of his theatres in favour of his sons, and,

❝in consideration of the natural love and affection which he hath for the said
three sons...doth give grant assign transfer and set over unto the said David
Fisher, Charles Fisher, and George Fisher, all and every the scenes, machines,
dresses, decorations and the properties, Books, goods, and chattels now
used in the theatres in the interest of the said David Fisher. ❞

There is some evidence that he did in fact delegate some of his managerial
duties to Charles, but the playbills bear witness that as a performer he never
retired at all, and was head of the company to the end.

Death of the founder

David Fisher I died in 1832 at Dereham, while the company was playing there. The last playbill to bear his name was for Friday, August 3rd, his own benefit night, for which was offered a triple bill consisting of a melodrama, *The Evil Eye*, an entertainment called *The Farmer's Daughter; or, The Force of Nature*, and a farce *The Illustrious Stranger*. Mr Fisher was billed to play in the first two of these and also to sing a comic song, and there is no reason to believe he did not fulfil his engagement. But it was his last. He died on Monday August 6th, aged 72. *The Norfolk Chronicle* paid this tribute to him:

❝As a manager he was esteemed, and by his indefatigable industry he has been enabled to leave his sons eleven theatres, many of which have been recently built and elegantly decorated. As an actor he displayed much talent. He was an affectionate parent and warm friend and in the strictest sense an honest, just and upright man. ❞

In the David Fisher Collection is a small drawing of his coffin, with the names of the officiating clergy, bearers and mourners – members of the company past and present, including the son of his old partner Scraggs, as well as three generations of the family. Behind them it is said that a procession a quarter of a mile long of carriages sent by his patrons followed his body to the churchyard, bearing witness to the high esteem in which he was held.

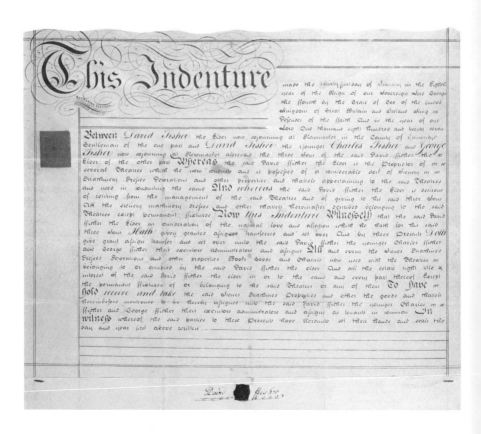

Indenture of 1827 recording David Fisher I's intention of handing over the management of the theatres to his sons David, Charles and George.

THEATRE, DEREHAM.

On FRIDAY the 3rd August, 1832.

For the Benefit of Mr. FISHER,

When will be produced for the First time at this Theatre, a grand Melo-Dramatic Play called the

EVIL EYE.

"THE EVIL EYE"—a common superstition in the Levant, and of which the imaginary effects are yet very singular on those who conceive themselves affected."

Lord Byron's Notes to the Giaour.

'Tis he ! 'tis he ! I know him now,
I know him by his pallid brow,
I know him by the "EVIL EYE !"
That aids his envious treachery ;

I know him by his jet-black barb,
Though not array'd in Arnant garb,
Apostate from his own vile faith
It shall not save him from the death.

Lord Byron's Giaour.

Mavroeyne, (the Waywode,) Mr. BELFOUR—Demetrius, Mr. RAY
Zanè Kiebabs, Mr. FISHER
Basilius, (Deposed Bey of Tripolitza,) Mr. TWIDDY
Andrea, } Sons of the Chieftain of the House of Abanitza, { Mr. C. FISHER, Jun.
Marco } { Master F. FISHER
Barozzi, (the Evil Eye,) Mr. HARGRAVE—Kara Mustapha, Mr. J. FISHER
Giorgio, Mr. HOLLIDAY—Attendant, Mr. IFE
Natives of Napoli, Soldiers, &c.
Helena, Mrs. C. FISHER—Phrosina, Miss CIBBER

IN THE COURSE OF THE PIECE THE FOLLOWING NEW SCENERY.

ORDER OF THE SCENERY.

Port of Napoli Di Romania.

Interior of the Dwelling of Demetrius.—Exterior of Ditto.

Defile of Rocks beneath the Dungeons of the Castle

EXCAVATION.

BOMBARDMENT, AND ANDREA'S VESSEL DISCOVERED AT ANCHOR.

SONG, MR. C. FISHER.

After which, a domestic Drama in two Acts, called the

Farmers Daughter,

OR THE FORCE OF NATURE

Farmer Acorn, Mr. RAY
George Acorn, (his brother supposed dead,) Mr. HARGRAVE
Fenton, Mr. J. FISHER
Charles Fenton, (Mate of the Albion,) Mr. BELFOUR
Mr. Twinkle, Mr. FISHER—Lawyer Glib, Mr. C. FISHER Jun.
Harrow, Mr. TWIDDY—Ploughwell, Mr. HOLLIDAY
Rustics, IFE, BROOKS
Mary Acorn, (the Farmer's, Daughter,) Miss CIBBER
Mrs. Twinkle, Mrs. C. FISHER

SONG MISS MORGAN.
COMIC SONG, BY MR. FISHER.

To conclude with the Laughable Farce of the

Illustrious STRANGER;

Or, MARRIED AND BURIED.

Aboulifar, Mr. HARGRAVE—Azan, Mr. BELFOUR—Alibajon, Mr. J. FISHER
Bowbell, Mr. C. FISHER, Jun.—Gimbo, Mr. RAY—Officer, Mr. HOLLIDAY
Guards, Nobles, Slaves, &c. &c.
irza, Miss CIBBER—Fatima, Mrs. C. FISHER

[Barker, Printer, Dereham.]

The last playbill to feature David Fisher I, three days before his death.

Pillans Esqr Revd Henson.

Mr Munford. Mr Philo.

Mr Page.

Mr Belfour. Mr Tweddle. Mr Hargreave. | Brooks. Care. Life. | *(coffin sketch with text)* | Sherriff. Middleton. Corr. Mr Bishop. | Mr Thorne. Mr Renf.

(on coffin) August. Burial. Died Augt 6 1832. Aged 72 years. Mr Fisher.

David & Betsy.

Charles & Fredk.

Mr & Mrs David.

Mr & Mrs Charles.

Mr & Mrs George.

Mr John & Mr George.

Mr & Mrs Howard.

Mr Scrags. Miss Cubber.

Mr Holliday & Mrs Hodgson.

Mr Gattey & Miss Morgan.

Mr & Mrs Nissing.

Sketch of David Fisher I's coffin with names of family and company mourners at his funeral on the 11th August, 1832.

The show goes on
It was on his second son, Charles, that the full management now descended.
There is a note in his hand on a slip of paper still kept by David Fisher's
great-great-great-granddaughter with two old quill pens, which reads:

❝Two Pens found in my Father's working-desk at his death, which both the week
before had been used by him. He died Monday Aug. 6. 1832.❞

But the circuit had never stopped long for anything, nor did it now. On the day
of the funeral, August 11th, Charles drew up the first page of the new salary list,
which he was to keep for the next decade.

David Fisher II
The eldest son, David Fisher II (1788–1858) was probably the most talented of the
second generation. He was a sufficiently outstanding actor to have been
engaged to replace the famous Edmund Kean in Shakespearean rôles in London
during the latter's illness in the autumn of 1817, and to be retained as a leading
member of the Drury Lane Company the following season, leaving only when
the death of his wife (leaving him with two small children) and the need for his
talents on the home circuit called him back to East Anglia. He was also an artist
of some talent, not only executing scenery and the interior decoration of some
of the theatres, but also painting remarkable family portraits, which still survive.
In addition he was leader of the Norwich Choral Society, and at one time taught
music and dancing. He had great charm, good looks and high spirits, and was
very attractive to women. He was married twice, but the lasting romantic
attachment of his life was to Mary Wilson, daughter of Baron Berners. They had
fallen in love when very young, but marriage between an actor and one of the
aristocracy was unthinkable, and both his and her parents forbade it. The
affection between them persisted, however. She never married, and, after his
second wife died, she looked after him to the end of his life. She survived him
by 16 years and provided for the education of his children and grand-children.
When she died she was buried by his side in Woodbridge churchyard.

Charles Fisher I
The second son, Charles (1792 – 1869), an outstanding singer and instrumentalist,
also made an appearance in London when, in 1818, he joined his elder brother
in the Drury Lane Company to play the lead in the comic opera *Lionel and
Clarissa,* for which his combined abilities as singer and actor well fitted him. He
was not, however, engaged as a regular member of the company, but returned
to the family circuit, where he not only acted, sang, and played, but assisted and
later succeeded his father as manager. He had in a remarkable degree the
musical talent which ran through the whole family. He played the violin, cello,
double bass, piano and organ – at one time wishing to leave the stage to
become a church organist. His nephew, David Fisher III, remembered him as
'a most eccentric fellow,' absorbed in successive enthusiasms, usually musical,
but sometimes for pursuits as different as conchology or picture collecting.
Towards the close of the circuit he left to become leader of the band in the
Norwich company, and later in other theatres. Finally he settled in Glasgow, as a
scene painter.

George Fisher
The third son, George (1793 – 1864), actor, musician, and printer to the
company, was of an academic bent, and left the circuit for some years to run a
school at Swaffham, for which his record of pupils' fees survives, though in a
somewhat mutilated condition. It is interesting to note that 'theatre' occurs as an

occasional item in the pupils' accounts. During his absence from the stage he also wrote an impressive *Companion and Key to the History of England. Consisting of Copious Genealogical Details of the British Sovereigns,* before returning to the company, of which he became manager after Charles left, remaining so until the circuit closed in 1844. He later compiled a *Harmony of the Gospels,* which was never published, but which still exists in his own manuscript. Like his brothers, he had married an actress, Marianne Nickless, who was also a member of the company. Both his and her portraits, painted by his brother David, have been preserved.

Henry Fisher
There was a fourth son, Henry (1794 – 1815), but he died young, though already showing the family talents for acting and music. As his nephew, David Fisher III, recalls:

'The brothers played quartets, changing all instruments round. Two of them (my father and Henry, who died early) being left-handed with their bows, owing to a slight lameness in left wrist. They were for many years connected with musical matters in Norwich. From the commencement of the festivals the name of Fisher will be found in the list of players. '

Elizabeth Fisher
There was also Elizabeth, born in 1790, Mr Fisher's 'pretty da'ter' as the Halesworth versifier called her, but she died just after Christmas in 1808. Though only 18 she had already made an impressive beginning on the stage. She was, said an obituary notice,

'a young lady of the most promising abilities, by whose premature death her parents have suffered an irreparable loss; her acquaintance a most worthy friend; and the stage a most distinguished ornament. '

The papers carried poetic tributes to her talent and beauty:

'Though now a lonely tenant of the tomb,
Fairer than opening roses was thy bloom.
Ah, who can paint the beauties of thine eye?
Who on a parents' stage thy place supply? '

8 The close of the circuit – and after

A country-wide recession in the theatre led to the closing of the Fisher Circuit in 1844, and all the theatres were sold. But the sound business basis on which they had been run meant that there were no debts to be settled at the end. The family went on to individual careers in the theatre and music. The third generation was now maturing. Charles's son, another Charles, made a famous name for himself as an actor in America, while David II's son, David III, made his reputation as comedian, straight actor and violinist, in Glasgow and London. Following him, two more Davids, his son and grandson, also became actors.

Centenary

In 1933, 101 years after David Fisher's death, a gathering of Fisher descendants and theatre enthusiasts came together in Dereham churchyard to celebrate the renewal of his headstone. After the ceremony, from the stage which he had built, his great-great-great-granddaughter, herself an actress and dancer, recited Henley's *Ballade of Dead Actors*. This was Mrs Kitty Shaw, who has now handed over to the Wells Centre, Wells-next-the-Sea, for exhibition, her family inheritance of the David Fisher Collection. The Charles Fisher Collection, which forms the rest of the exhibition, comes from Miss Caroline Fisher Carver, also a great-great-great-granddaughter of David Fisher I, through his son George.

Ceremony for the renewal of David Fisher I's gravestone in Dereham churchyard in 1933, organised by his great-granddaughter, Ruth Carver (née Fisher), seen here behind the headstone.

Appendix: The collections

The David Fisher collection

● Playbills

Bungay
1794 June 5–14 (3 bills)
1796 Mch 10 – May 17 (23)
1799–1800 Dec 28 – Mch 1 (22)
1801–02 Dec 22 – Jan 8 (6)
1804 Jan 3 – Mch 10 (26)
1806 Jan 9 – Mch 8 (24)
1809–10 Dec 1 – Jan 27 (25)
1811–12 Nov 14 – Jan 9 (19)
1822 Jan 5 (1)
1823–24 Dec 8 – Feb 5 (26)
1828 Feb 28 – May 1 (35)
1832 Jan 28 – Mch 10 (16)
1833–34 Nov 30 – Jan 27 (38)
1836 Jan 11 – Mch 3 (31)
1840 Feb 10–11 (2)

Dereham
1832 July 30 – Aug 3 (3)
1845 Apr 25 (1)
1871 June 26 (2)

London: Drury Lane
1849 Dec 26 (1)
1850 Feb 28 (1)
1871 Sept 27 (1)

London: Princess's
1846 Apr 17 – May 12 (2)
1851 May 5 – July 14 (3)

Newmarket
1831 Dec 23 (1)
1845 Nov 28 (1)

North Walsham
1828 May 31 – June 30 (16)
1830 Apr 13 – June 16 (22)
1832 May 24–25 (2)
1836 Apr 16–18 (2)
1838 June 14 (1)

Norwich
1857 Apr 17 (1)
1863 Dec 9–11 (2)

Swaffham
1830 Nov 1 (1)

Wells
1834 Apr 5 (1)
1836 May 28 – June 27 (13)

Woodbridge
1823 Feb 15 (1)

Yarmouth
1845 Aug 22 (1)

● Other printed material
  The Royal Bible, 1761, in oak box.
  Benefit ticket of Mr and Mrs D Fisher.
  Music Hath Charms, by David Fisher III.
  Press notices of David Fisher III, 1849–55.
  Press cuttings, 19th and 20th centuries.
  Song:*The British Volunteers!* By David Fisher III, 1863.
  Salaries list and cash book, Theatre Royal, Edinburgh, 1870.
  The Norfolk and Suffolk Company of Comedians and the Fisher Family by
  James Carver, 1909.
  Programme of Birmingham Repertory Theatre, 4 June 1927.
  Fisher Family tree.
  East Anglian Theatre, catalogue of exhibition in Castle Museum, Norwich,
  1952.

● Manuscript material.
  Indenture assigning David Fisher's theatrical property to his sons, 1827.
  Copy of court roll admitting Thomas Sadler to copyhold tenancy of
  Woodbridge Theatre, 1833.
  Management notebooks, 1832.
  Salaries list, 1832–42.
  George Fisher:
     benefit book.1823–39,
     record of income from school fees, 1828–36,
     Harmony of the Gospels
  Play script, *Castle of de Courcy* by W P Isaacson, 1843.
  Letters from David Fisher II, Charles Fisher I, George Fisher and others.
  Biographical notes.

● Portraits
  Engraving of David Fisher II, 1817.
  Colour print of David Fisher III's second wife.
  Photographs of Charles Fisher I, George Fisher, David Fisher III, David Fisher
  IV and others.

● Other items.
  Quill pen used by David Fisher I
  Red Sulphur of seal of Garrick and Shakespeare by Nathaniel Marchant;
  belonging to David Fisher I;
  Sketch of David Fisher I's funeral order.

The Charles Fisher collection

● Playbills

New York: Academy of Music
1855 Apr 10 (1)

New York: Bowery
1856 June 30 – July 10 (2)

New York: Broadway
1856 June 13 (1)

New York: Burton's
1856 Sept 1 – Dec 8 (3)
1857 Oct 1–26 (2)
1858 Jan 18 (1)
undated (3)

New York: Wallack's
1862 Jan 23 – Oct 24 (18)
1863 Jan 2 – Dec 10 (35)
1864 Feb 22 – Nov 25 (14)
1865 Jan 9 – June 12 (15)

● Programmes

Boston: Boston Museum
1874 (1)

Buffalo: Academy of Music
1882 Jan 9 – Jan 11 (2)

Erie, PA: Park Opera House
1882 Apr 15–25 (2)

New York: Booth's
1877 Dec 22–26 (2)

New York: Daly's
1880 Sept 21 (1)

St Louis: Olympic
1882 Jan 30 – Feb 5 (1)

● Photographs
Charles Fisher II (33); his daughter Jane (1)
Wells theatre in the 1950s

● Other items
Scrap album of Charles Fisher II, 1871–83
Stage replica of masonic apron belonging to George Fisher

Bibliography

Burley, T L G *Playhouses and Players of East Anglia.*
Jarrold, Norwich, 1928.

Carver, James. *The Norfolk and Suffolk Company of Comedians and the Fisher Family. A Chapter in Heredity.*
A paper read before the Norwich Science Gossip Club on March 10th, 1909.

Field, Moira. 'The Fishers on the Lamplit Stage.'
East Anglian Magazine,
September 1981 pp 504–507.

Grice, Elizabeth. *Rogues and Vagabonds; or The Actors' Road to Respectability.*
Dalton, Lavenham, 1977.

'The Old Circuits, by a Septuagenarian.' *The Theatre,* 1 April 1880 pp 193–199.
With reminiscences by David Fisher III.

Reid, Francis. 'A Museum of Fishers.'
Cue: Technical Theatre Review, July–August 1981 pp 18–19.